THE STORY OF
SMALL PINE

by Diane Stortz
Illustrated by Mary Lou Faltico

All young pine trees long
to grow up straight and tall
so they can be Christmas
trees when they are older.

Small Pine was more than a little crooked and not tall at all. But even when he was sold for half price at an after-Christmas sale, Small Pine never stopped hoping. "Someday I will be a Christmas tree," he said. "I know I will."

Small Pine was planted
in a corner of the backyard.
He learned to be happy
there, mostly because of
a little boy named John
Michael.

On spring days, John Michael sat quietly and watched a pair of robins make a nest in Small Pine's branches.

On hot summer days, he lay in Small Pine's shade to keep cool.

On fall days, he and his
puppy Nappy played ball
together in Small Pine's
corner of the backyard.

And on winter days,
when soft snow covered the
ground, John Michael made
perfect snow angels all
around Small Pine.

With winter and the first snow, Small Pine knew Christmas would be coming soon. He stood as straight and tall as he possibly could, still hoping that somehow he would be a Christmas tree.

But another taller,
straighter tree stood in John
Michael's house, decorated
with lights and ornaments.

On Christmas morning, John Michael tiptoed downstairs. Under the tree were so many presents! But through the window, as the sun was coming up, John Michael saw something even more wonderful.

It was Small Pine, covered with new snow, glistening like a hundred lights. A family of redbirds rested on his branches, and the sun shone like a starburst at the top of the little tree.

"Small Pine, you're a Christmas tree!" said John Michael. Small Pine proudly stood as straight and tall as he possibly could. He was very, very happy!